AR ok
Grade - 3.9
point - 1.0

SCHOOL SPIRIT SABOTAGE

Also by Elizabeth Levy

GORGONZOLA ZOMBIES IN THE PARK

KEEP MS. SUGARMAN IN THE
FOURTH GRADE

DRACULA IS A PAIN IN THE NECK

FRANKENSTEIN MOVED IN
ON THE FOURTH FLOOR

A Brian and Pea Brain Mystery

SCHOOL SPIRIT SABOTAGE

by ELIZABETH LEVY

illustrated by George Ulrich

HarperCollins*Publishers*

Library of Congress Cataloging-in-Publication Data
Levy, Elizabeth.
  School spirit sabotage : a Brian and Pea Brain mystery / by Elizabeth
Levy ; illustrated by George Ulrich.
    p.   cm.
  Summary: Brian and his younger sister Penny try to catch the mis-
chievous person who has been sabotaging School Spirit Week.
  ISBN 0-06-023407-5. — ISBN 0-06-023408-3 (lib. bdg.)
  [1. Schools—Fiction. 2. Brothers and sisters—Fiction. 3. Mystery
and detective stories.] I. Ulrich, George, ill. II. Title.
PZ7.L5827Sc 1994   93-23029
[Fic]—dc20   CIP
                                                      AC

Typography by Elynn Cohen
1   2   3   4   5   6   7   8   9   10

First Edition

To Larry—
my very own Brian Brain
from his sister Pea Brain

Contents

1

Monday

Clash Bash

"Ma," screamed Brian, as he and his sister ran down the stairs into the kitchen. "Pea Brain's dressed herself again this morning. Do something!"

Brian's sister, Penny, was dressed in yellow, purple, and green, with one bright-orange sock on her left foot and one chartreuse sock on her right. Penny was in kindergarten, and she had just begun to pick out her own clothes.

"You look like a neon sign! You'll stop traffic! You'll blind the bus driver," warned Brian. Brian was wearing a light-brown shirt and khaki pants.

"Penny, honey, are you sure you want to wear all those colors?" asked Mr. Casanova.

"Dad, it's School Spirit Week," said Penny. "We're supposed to wear bright clothes!"

"There's bright and there's bright," said Mr. Casanova.

Mrs. Casanova went to the refrigerator and looked at a sheet of paper under a magnet.

Dear Pine Beach Parent,

The second week of school will be School Spirit Week. The high spirits and sense of community sparked by S.S.W. last throughout the school year and help make Pine

2

Beach an enriching experience for all. We urge all parents to help and encourage their children to dress up and take an active part in the week's festivities.

MONDAY — CLASH BASH
Anything that doesn't go goes
★
TUESDAY — 1950s DAY
★
WEDNESDAY — YAD SDRAWKCAB
Backwards Day
★
THURSDAY — DRESS-UP DAY
Formal is the word
★
FRIDAY — ANIMAL HULLABALOO
*Dress up as your favorite animal for
a day that is a real zoo*

Thank you all for your cooperation.

Sincerely,
Charles Demert
School Principal

"I forgot about School Spirit Week," said Mrs. Casanova. "Brian, it says here that today you're supposed to clash."

"See?" said Penny. "I'm dressed right. You look like a tree trunk."

"School Spirit Week is stupid," said Brian.

"Is not!"

"The only ones who get excited about School Spirit Week are the permanently stupid."

Penny glared at him. "I'm going to take Flea to school—because she's bright too." Flea was the Casanovas' orange cat. Mrs. Casanova had found her at a church flea market. Flea was licking her paw, but she looked up at the sound of her name.

"Flea can't go to school, Pea Brain. They don't allow animals," said Brian.

"Brian's right, Penny," said Mrs. Casanova. "Animals don't belong in school."

4

"They do in our class—we have a hundred tadpoles, two guinea pigs, and a thousand butterflies."

"You don't have a thousand butterflies—you've got a mess of dried cocoons—they *never* hatch. Trust me! I've been through kindergarten," said Brian.

"They're going to hatch the last day of School Spirit Week. It'll be a thousand wings for old Pine Beach." Penny moved her hands through the air like a butterfly's wings.

"It'll be a thousand dead butterflies, Pea Brain."

"Brian, don't call her Pea Brain," said Mrs. Casanova. "And no talk about dead butterflies at the breakfast table."

"You kids had better get out to the curb," said Mr. Casanova. "The school bus will be coming." He handed them their lunches.

6

Penny put on her bright-orange jacket, which clashed with her neon-yellow pants. She headed out the door. Her jacket was very lumpy.

The bus rolled up, and Brian helped Penny up the big step.

"Take a seat, Pea Brain," he said.

"Why do you call her Pea Brain? She's so cute," asked Heather Hamilton, a girl in Brian's class. Heather was wearing a banana-yellow shirt, fire-engine-red pants, and green socks.

"Brian thinks he's such a brain," said Penny. "But he's not. He forgot Clash Day!"

Brian rolled his eyes. "When she was little, she couldn't say Brian," he explained to Heather. "She kept calling me Brain."

"That's so adorable," said Heather.

Brian made a face. Heather was a

7

gusher. Brian thought she gushed a little too much. She was new to the school, even though her mom was the school secretary at Pine Beach.

She and her mom used to live in another district, but they had recently moved so that Mrs. Hamilton could be closer to her job.

Penny sat down next to Virginia, her best friend in kindergarten. Virginia was wearing three different kinds of plaids. "My brother forgot Clash Day," said Penny. She loved feeling smarter than Brian.

The bus pulled up to the school, and the principal, Mr. Demert, greeted each busload outside by the flagpole. He was dressed in a plaid jacket, lime-green pants, a tie shaped like a goldfish, and a huge orange-blue-and-green stocking cap that went all the way down to his ankles

with a little bell on the end. Mr. Demert loved hats. He was bald, and he claimed he'd do anything to keep his "noggin" covered. Heather's mom was standing next to Mr. Demert dressed in a bright orange-and-black-plaid suit, red shoes, and neon-green sunglasses.

"Good morning, girls and boys," said Mr. Demert. "Welcome to School Spirit Week. We always have it the second week of school so that our new children can learn a very important lesson about Pine Beach School. What is that lesson?!"

"Pine Beach School is the greatest!" shouted Mrs. Hamilton. She had a very loud voice. Heather looked a little embarrassed.

Mr. Demert waved his hat. "Well, I think it is," he said. "School is hard work, but people have to get along and have fun. And so, in that spirit, every day this week we will celebrate in a different way. Today is the day that anything that doesn't go goes. After you go to your classrooms and after your first lesson, we will meet out on the playground for the Clash Bash."

Brian and Penny walked into school together. Brian walked Penny to the kindergarten class. Since this was only Penny's second week at school, Brian figured she still could get lost.

"Good morning, Brian," said his teacher, Mr. Vickers, who was talking to Penny's teacher, Ms. Turnaturi. Mr. Vickers was a new teacher this year. He had a high forehead, and he was very, very neat. Brian liked him, although the other kids in the class thought that he was too strict. He was dressed in gray pants and a black shirt.

Brian and Mr. Vickers walked back to

their class together.

"Mr. Vickers," said Heather, who was already in her seat. "Brian isn't dressed for Clash Day! My old school had a great School Spirit Week. Everybody dressed really wild."

"You think everything was better at your old school," said Mookie. "Besides, Brian's wearing two different shades of brown."

"Brown is a color," said Brian. "It's a very fine color. It's the color of a small brown fawn—it's the color of the sand."

"That's beautiful, Brian," said Mr. Vickers.

"But sir!" complained Heather. "Brian doesn't clash. The Clemente School, my old school, had the true school spirit."

"Then why does your mother work here?" taunted Jennifer.

Mr. Vickers's mouth turned down. "That's enough, class. Personally, I think that to devote an entire week to school spirit is silly, a travesty."

"Something that hangs on the wall?" asked Mookie.

Mr. Vickers scowled. "That's a tapestry. A travesty is a mockery, a farce, a joke. School should not be a joke. Too much fun is a dangerous thing," said Mr. Vickers. "Please open your math books."

After math and science, Mr. Demert showed up at the door to Mr. Vickers's class.

"It's time for your class to move out for the parade of colors."

As the school moved onto the playground, the band played terrible-sounding music. The clarinets all squeaked, the drums banged only on the off beat, and the tubas honked whenever they felt like it. Mr. Demert wanted the music to really clash.

Mr. Demert grinned and conducted

the band as if it were the most melodious music in the world. Mr. Vickers put his fingers in his ears.

Just as the clarinet hit a particularly squeaky note, Brian noticed Penny and her class. Penny's jacket was still lumpy. Penny clutched her stomach. Brian wondered if she was sick. He started to walk toward her when something orange and furry flew out from under her bright-orange jacket and pounced on the bell of Mr. Demert's hat. The hat sailed off Mr. Demert's head, revealing his very bald head.

"Oh no, Flea!" muttered Brian.

Mr. Demert grabbed for his hat and whirled around to see who had taken it. Flea panicked and began running full tilt toward the sandbox. Brian took off after her. Penny ran too, but Brian was faster.

Brian dove for Flea and came up with

a mouthful of sand. He grabbed Flea and held on tight.

"Uh-oh," whispered Penny. "I think I'm in trouble."

Brian tried to get the sand out of his mouth. He glared at his little sister. The whole school started to come toward them, led by Mr. Demert and Mr. Vickers.

"What is that cat doing here, Brian Casanova?" yelled Mr. Demert as he crossed the playground. He motioned for them to get out of the sandbox.

Penny's knees were shaking. "Don't panic, Pea Brain," whispered Brian. "I'll take care of this."

"I'm gonna be kicked out of kindergarten," wailed Penny. "Flea was asleep all morning. Ms. Turnaturi never even knew she was there."

"Shh," said Brian as Mr. Demert and

16

the others leaned into the sandbox.

"Brian," said Mr. Demert. "You are the last person I would expect to disrupt school in this way."

Brian sighed. "I'm sorry, Mr. Demert. I shouldn't have brought my cat to school, but I thought she belonged because it's Clash Day," said Brian.

"I could kiss you," whispered Penny.

"Don't," warned Brian.

Mr. Demert shook his head. "Brian, you know better than to bring a cat to school."

"Please don't kick Brian out because of this," sobbed Penny. "If my brother gets kicked out of school, I want to get kicked out too."

"I don't think we'll need to go that far," said Mr. Demert. "Brian, I want you to promise me that nothing like this will happen again."

Brian lowered his head. "Yes, sir," he said. Heather was giggling. Brian figured she was giggling because he was in trouble. Brian hated being in trouble.

2

Tuesday

1950s Day

"Brian! I need help!" said Penny the next morning. She pounded on the bathroom door.

Brian put down his comb and sighed. He opened the door. "What now?"

"My hair," said Penny. "Mom and Dad are busy. Help me." Penny had tried to put her hair into a ponytail. Unfortunately, Penny had put the ponytail on the very top of her head. Her hair stuck up like a paintbrush.

"I don't do hair," said Brian.

Mr. Casanova walked by. "Is today the day you're supposed to go to school with weird hair?" he asked innocently when he saw Penny.

Penny gave him a dirty look. "I'm supposed to look frosty," she said. "It's 1950s Day in School Spirit Week."

"Frosty?" asked Mr. Casanova.

"You know—super—excellent."

"I think she means 'cool,'" said Brian.

"What a pinhead!"

"Yeah, well, you don't look very cool either," said Penny, following Brian and her father down the stairs and into the kitchen. "I thought you were dressing up like Elvis," she said. She had vowed to herself to be nice to Brian for a whole week for what he had done for her, but he wasn't making it easy.

Brian was wearing his chinos and fake glasses. "I'm Buddy Holly. He's a rock star you probably never heard of. Besides, the principal always dresses up as Elvis. Last year Mr. Demert wore an Elvis outfit that was just ridiculous," said Brian. "He sweated all day."

"Oh, I can't wait to see the principal sweat," said Penny. "I wonder if his bald head perspires."

"He wears a goofy wig, Pea Brain," said Brian. "You never see his bald head

21

sweat during School Spirit Week."

Brian and Penny went out to wait for the school bus. When they got to school, Brian took Penny to her class again. Penny's teacher, Ms. Turnaturi, was dressed in a big circle skirt with rhinestones spelling out her first name, Gabriella. She had rhinestones on the collar of her shirt too.

"You look beautiful," said Penny.

Ms. Turnaturi twirled around, making the rhinestones dance. "Today we're going to do arithmetic by counting the rhinestones."

Brian walked to his class. He thought counting rhinestones sounded very babyish.

When Brian got to his class, he saw that Mr. Vickers was wearing a suit with a narrow tie. Heather was wearing bobby socks and a cute little pleated plaid skirt.

Mr. Vickers rapped on the board with his pointer. "The 1950s is an era we should all respect," he said. "Can anybody guess who I'm dressed as?"

"Richard Nixon?" asked Mookie.

Mr. Vickers frowned. "No, I'm a rock star."

"Buddy Holly," said Brian. He grinned.

"Right, Brian." Mr. Vickers smiled. Mr. Vickers taught a history lesson on the 1950s. He talked about the early civil-rights movement and the origins of rock music in black southern soul and blues. When he finished his lesson, he said, "I need somebody to go to the principal's office for me. Heather, will you take these papers to your mother?"

Heather blushed. She hated to be singled out because her mother worked at the school. "I'm supposed to be hall monitor for the kindergarten," she said.

"All right. Brian, will you please take my attendance sheets to Mr. Demert's office?" He handed the papers to Brian. "You and Heather can both meet us in the assembly."

Brian and Heather headed off together. "I love being the monitor in the kindergarten corridor," said Heather. "The kindergartners are so cute."

As they passed the open door to the kindergarten, Ms. Turnaturi was lining up Penny's class for assembly. "The teachers are going to rock around the clock for the whole school," said Ms. Turnaturi.

"Yay!" shouted all the kindergartners.

Brian thought it was stupid to be so excited.

Ms. Turnaturi put her finger to her lips. "Be careful. You don't want to wake the butterflies before their time.

It's important that they be left alone these last few days. Nobody should touch them."

Brian stared at the caterpillar cage. He could remember his own caterpillars in kindergarten. He had told Penny the truth—not one had hatched. It had been very sad. Penny didn't notice Brian standing in the doorway.

She walked cautiously to the oblong glass container that had once held the caterpillars and now held the cocoons. The cocoons looked very quiet. In fact, they looked dead.

"Are you sure they're alive?" Penny asked, sounding worried.

"They'll be fine," said Ms. Turnaturi. "Come on, Penny. It's time for the assembly."

Penny gave the cocoons one more worried look. She glanced up and saw that

Brian was standing in the hallway. She wondered what he was doing there.

Brian shook himself. He didn't have time to be thinking about dead caterpillars. He hurried past Heather in the hall and delivered the papers to the principal's empty office. Then he rushed to the assembly.

Mr. Demert was already onstage, dressed in a bright-red jumpsuit with a high collar inset with bright beads. He had gold chains around his waist and a silk scarf around his neck.

He looked just like the pictures of Elvis, except for one problem. His bald head.

"Where's his wig?" Penny whispered.

"Shh," said Ms. Turnaturi. "Pretend you don't notice."

Soon everybody in the auditorium was whispering, even though Mr. Demert

was doing his best to try to dance and shake his body like Elvis.

"A bald Elvis doesn't cut it," Mookie whispered to Brian.

Mr. Demert stopped his dancing. He took the microphone. He coughed into it. "A few of you might notice that I don't look exactly like Elvis," he said.

The entire school started to titter.

"Somebody has stolen my Elvis wig from my office. I suppose somebody thought he or she was being funny. I don't think so. School Spirit Week should not be spoiled by silly pranks. I will give the culprit until the end of the day to come forward without fear of punishment. And now let the festivities continue."

The P.A. system wailed out "You ain't nothin' but a hound dog." Ms. Turnaturi came out with a droopy-eyed basset hound on a leash.

All the teachers danced around Mr. Demert, swiveling their hips. But all in all, Mookie was right—a bald Elvis just didn't cut it.

As they were leaving the assembly, Penny's and Brian's classes ended up in the hallway together.

Mr. Vickers whispered something to Ms. Turnaturi. She laughed. Then she took her place at the front of the kindergarten class line.

Ms. Turnaturi stopped at the door to make sure that all of the stragglers got into the class. Penny walked into the kindergarten classroom first. She put her hand to her mouth.

"Oh, no!" she shrieked. Something black and bushy sat inside the glass container holding all of the cocoons. "An animal is trying to eat our butterflies!" The

other kindergartners began to scream.

Ms. Turnaturi took a step forward and lifted up the glass top. She reached in and brought out the Elvis wig. One of the cocoons had gotten entangled in Elvis's bangs.

Ms. Turnaturi frowned. She pulled the cocoon off Elvis's hair and put it gently back in the glass box.

"Does anybody know how this wig got

in with the cocoons?" she asked, holding the wig up high.

Penny looked around the room. She tried to think of who might be trying to ruin School Spirit Week. Brian had said that School Spirit Week was stupid. And he certainly knew about the cocoons. He was the one who had said they would never hatch. He had also called Mr. Demert's wig goofy. Plus she had seen him in the hall right outside their class.

Brian could be the culprit.

Ms. Turnaturi clapped her hands. "Penny," she said, "you're daydreaming. It's time to do your workbook."

Penny opened her workbook, but all she could think about was Brian. All day she tried to concentrate, but even during story hour her mind wandered. She thought of Brian being kicked out of school and sent to jail—all for a stolen wig.

During the last lesson period, Mr. Vickers gave the second graders an arithmetic test. Brian was working too hard to worry about cocoons or wigs.

As they passed the exams to the front, Heather turned to Brian. "Did you hear about where they found Elvis's wig?" she asked.

"Heather," said Mr. Vickers, "if I wanted you to talk while I'm picking up the exams, I would have told you."

Heather looked upset. "Nobody ever yelled at me at my old school," she mumbled.

"I didn't yell at you," said Mr. Vickers. "I corrected you. There is a difference."

"I thought that during School Spirit Week things would be a little more fun," said Heather with a pout. "It was at the Clemente School."

Mr. Vickers frowned at the word

"fun." "I presume all of you heard that Mr. Demert's wig was found. I do not think that putting Elvis wigs into the butterfly-cocoon cage in kindergarten is fun," he said sternly.

"Is that where it was found?" asked Brian. He *hadn't* heard exactly. Suddenly Brian stopped worrying about his arithmetic test. Now he was worried about Penny.

He remembered telling Penny that the cocoons would never hatch. What if she had put the Elvis wig in there to keep them warm? He had seen Penny in her classroom. But what if she had gotten permission to go to the bathroom right before he had seen her? That would have been before Heather was monitoring the hall before the assembly. The hall could have been empty. What if Penny had snuck into the principal's office and taken it herself? It was just the kind of hair-brained scheme that Penny might think up.

Brian groaned to himself.

"Brian," asked Mr. Vickers, "are you all right?"

Brian nodded. But he knew one thing. Penny would have been too chicken to take Mr. Demert's wig by herself. She would have to have had an accomplice. Brian was going to have to be a detective to find out who was putting his little sister up to ruining School Spirit Week.

He screwed up his eyes.

"Is there a reason why you're looking cross-eyed?" asked Mookie.

Brian sighed. This was work for a brain—a real brain. He just hoped that he was up to the job.

4

Wednesday

yaD sdrawkcaB

The next morning, Brian was determined to make sure that Penny did not get into any more trouble. Penny was equally sure that she had to watch Brian so that he didn't get kicked out of school. They eyed each other suspiciously over the breakfast table.

Brian frowned at Penny. Her shirt was buttoned in the back. She got up to get cereal and walked backward, doing a kind of sideways shuffle that zigzagged across the kitchen. She almost stepped on Flea.

"Why are you walking like that?" Brian asked.

"My jeans fit funny," Penny admitted. "It kind of hurts to have my jeans on backward."

Brian rolled his eyes. "You're supposed to wear backward clothes big," he said. "Didn't you know that?"

Penny shook her head. "How was I supposed to find out? I'm only in kindergarten," she said. "There's lots of stuff that I don't know."

Brian sighed. He went back to his bedroom and pulled out a pair of jeans. "Here. My jeans will be big on you. Wear them."

"That was very nice, Brian," said Mrs. Casanova. Brian blushed. He hated it when his mom caught him being nice to

Penny. Penny came back wearing Brian's jeans. They drooped in the front, but she looked a lot more comfortable.

"Do I look too stupid?" she asked.

Brian shook his head. "You look good."

"What are *you* wearing backward, Brian?" Penny asked. Brian put on his baseball cap with the bill facing backward. Penny took Brian's hand to walk to the curb.

"Brian, promise me you won't do anything terrible today?" she asked.

"What are you talking about?"

"You know, like taking the principal's wig," said Penny.

Brian stared at her. "You mean you didn't take the principal's wig yourself?"

"Me!" exclaimed Penny. "I'm just a little kid."

Brian didn't know whether to believe

her or not. But it got him thinking. Maybe he had been too quick to decide it was Penny. After all, there weren't any clues that pointed to Penny. That's what he needed—clues. Like finding somebody with the hair of Elvis's wig on their clothes . . . in mysteries detectives were always finding stray hairs.

Brian sighed when he got on the bus. All of the kids were wearing their clothes backward, and nobody was wearing the 1950s clothes he or she had worn yesterday. This clue business was tougher than it looked.

When they got to school, the bell rang for dismissal, and all the clocks said 3 P.M.

"Good-bye, boys and girls," said Heather's mom as she arrived for work. "I hope you have a nice afternoon."

"Your mom really gets into School

Spirit Week, doesn't she?" said Brian.

"What do you mean?" asked Heather. She sounded mad.

"I just meant that she must really like this school," said Brian, wondering why Heather was so huffy.

"She does," said Heather.

"Brian," begged Penny, tugging on his sleeve, "be careful."

"About what, Pea Brain?" snapped Brian.

Penny sighed. She wanted to warn him not to do anything stupid to ruin Backwards Day. But Brian would never listen to her.

Brian walked Penny to her class. "Aren't we supposed to walk backward?" Penny asked.

Brian sighed. He took her hand and walked backward.

"Good-bye, Penny," he said at the

kindergarten door.

"You mean 'Hello,'" said Penny. "Everything should be backward today."

Brian rolled his eyes. He left Penny at the kindergarten door. Ms. Turnaturi was standing with her back to the class. "Girls and boys, line up for dismissal."

Penny and Virginia looked at each other. "Are we really supposed to go home?" Penny asked.

"No," said Ms. Turnaturi. "It's just a joke. At the end of the day we'll have show and tell and end with the Pledge of Allegiance. Everything today is backward."

"It's tell and show. You should say it backward," said Penny.

Ms. Turnaturi smiled, but Penny thought that maybe she shouldn't have corrected her teacher.

Backwards Day was very confusing for

41

everybody. In the halls the teachers had to be very careful because everybody was walking backward and knocking into each other like tumbling dice in a game of Chutes and Ladders.

The kindergartners took their nap before lunch instead of after, since this was Backwards Day. Penny lay down on the rug feeling very wide awake. She stared at the cocoons' cage.

If the cocoons started going backward in time, they'd turn into caterpillars instead of butterflies.

Penny imagined the entire kindergarten class being haunted by ghost butterflies who flew backward. She rubbed her eyes and shivered. She had to know if the cocoons were really dead. Everyone around her looked asleep. Even Ms. Turnaturi had her head on her desk.

Penny got up off her rug. She lifted

the top of the container and put her hand into the glass container and touched one of the cocoons. It felt papery and dry as dust.

"Penny," said Ms. Turnaturi quietly, lifting her head. "Leave the cocoons alone. I've told you many times that it's important that they not be touched during the last few days."

"I don't think they like going backward," whispered Penny.

Ms. Turnaturi smiled as if Penny were making a joke. But she wasn't.

At the end of the day Mr. Vickers reminded Brian's class that it was their turn to go to the principal's office and help with the morning announcements. Every day Mr. Demert asked students from a different class to help him make the morning announcements. Today it was the second grade's turn.

"Although why the morning announcements matter now that the day is over, I don't know," muttered Mr. Vickers.

"On yaD sdrawkcaB, it's the way the school day traditionally ends," said Mookie.

"Some traditions are silly," said Mr. Vickers. Mr. Vickers walked at the front of the class to the principal's office. Brian walked straight ahead with Mr. Vickers. Mookie bumped into a table in the hallway and nearly fell down. The table crashed to the floor.

"Are you all right?" Mr. Vickers asked.

Mookie rubbed the back of his head. "yakO," he said.

Mr. Vickers looked puzzled. "That's 'okay' backward," whispered Brian. Mr. Vickers rolled his eyes.

When they got to the principal's office,

Mr. Demert greeted them. "Good morning, Mr. Vickers and Class 201. Here's the tape of the Pledge and 'The Star-Spangled Banner.' Brian has never made the announcements over the P.A. before. Why don't you do it?"

Brian licked his lips. Talking in public made him very nervous.

Mr. Demert handed the tape of the Pledge and "The Star-Spangled Banner" to Mr. Vickers, who handed it to Mookie, who handed it to Heather, who handed it to Brian. Brian's hands were so sweaty that he dropped it. Heather and Mookie both reached for it. It fell under Mr. Demert's desk. Heather picked it up and handed it to Mookie, who gave it to Brian.

"Brian, remember to remind everyone that tomorrow is Dress-Up Day," said Mr. Demert. "I'll be wearing my top hat, which I am keeping under lock and key."

Brian's palms still felt sweaty. He put the cassette in the machine.

Brian spoke into the microphone. "Good afternoon, everybody," he said. His voice sounded squeaky.

"Ahem," said Mr. Demert. "Good *morning!*"

"Whoops," said Brian. "Good morning," he corrected himself. "Would everybody please rise for the Pledge of Allegiance and the singing of the national anthem?"

In her kindergarten class Penny put her hand over her heart. She heard her brother's voice come over the P.A. His voice sounded squeaky—the way it did when he was very nervous. Penny giggled nervously. She always got nervous when Brian was tense.

Then over the loudspeaker came another voice. This voice didn't even sound

47

human. It sounded like it was underwater. "All for justice and liberty with indivisible God under nation one stands it which for republic the to and America of States United the of flag the to allegiance pledge I."

In the principal's office Mr. Demert started sputtering. Brian looked panic-stricken. Mr. Demert grabbed the microphone from Brian. "Excuse me, boys and girls, that Pledge should never have been said backward. I want these pranks to stop. If I catch the person who has been fooling with School Spirit Week, he or she will be in serious trouble."

Heather's mother came running into the office. "What's wrong?"

"Somebody is making a mockery of School Spirit Week."

"A tapestry," said Heather.

Her mother stared at her.

Mr. Demert took the tape out of the machine. "Mookie," he said, "why don't you lead the school in the real Pledge."

Mookie stepped up to the microphone. "I pledge allegiance to the flag . . ."

"I didn't do it, Mr. Demert, honest," said Brian. "I just put in the tape that you gave us."

Mr. Demert scratched his bald head. "This is a case of a little too much school spirit," he said, frowning. "I want it to stop."

"One school spirit too many," muttered Brian. The voice on the tape had been very weird sounding, but was it a girl or a boy? It was so garbled, Brian couldn't tell who it was.

But Brian knew one thing.

Somebody had to have prepared the tape in advance.

Mookie? Mookie never even planned

what he was going to watch on TV. It didn't seem like Mookie.

Heather? Heather was new to the school. Why her?

Brian sighed. He couldn't believe how hard it was to find clues. He had a feeling there was a clue right under his nose, but he couldn't find it.

Mr. Vickers interrupted his thoughts. "Brian," he said, "Backwards Day is finally over." He looked out the window of the principal's office. "Your sister is waiting for you."

Brian looked up. He wondered if Mr. Vickers suspected *him*.

Brian walked out to the buses. Penny tugged on his arm as they climbed onto the bus. "Tell me you didn't do it," she whispered. "Please."

"Pea Brain, leave me alone," muttered Brian.

Penny crossed her arms over her chest. Her lower lip stuck out.

"Cheer up, Penny," said Mookie. "Tomorrow's Dress-Up Day. Maybe all your cocoons will hatch into beautiful butterflies. Did you know my grandmother collects butterflies?"

"What's all this talk about butterflies?" asked Heather.

"The kindergarten cocoons are ready to hatch," explained Penny.

"How can you guys talk about butterflies? We three are all suspects for messing with the pledge," said Brian.

"We have to be very quiet in class and not touch the cocoons," said Virginia, ignoring him. "And then we're going to set them free on the last day of School Spirit Week."

"Oh sure," muttered Brian. "And the Easter Bunny is real."

Penny's eyes widened. "The Easter Bunny *is* real," she said.

"What do you think Mr. Demert will do if he catches the person who's been doing the pranks?" interrupted Heather.

"Boil him or her in oil," said Mookie.

Heather made a face. "Don't you think the person who did this will be kicked out of school?" she asked.

"Probably," said Brian.

Penny stared at him. It had been his voice she had heard just before the backward Pledge came on. Penny swallowed hard. She really didn't want Brian to get kicked out of school. It would put their parents in a very bad mood.

4

Thursday

Puttin' On My Top Hat

The next morning Penny came down to breakfast wearing a pink and white dress with blue ribbons. She had worn it to her cousin Marta's wedding. She twirled in front of Brian, who was dressed in a baggy T-shirt and jeans. He was writing at the breakfast table.

"Are you doing your homework at the last minute?" she asked.

Brian shook his head. "I'm solving a mystery," he said. "I need quiet. All great detectives need quiet."

Penny looked over Brian's shoulder. He had made a chart and he was using different color markers.

He had written:

SUSPECTS:	ACCESS:	MOTIVE:
Mookie		
Heather		
Mr. Demert		
Mr. Vickers		
Penny		

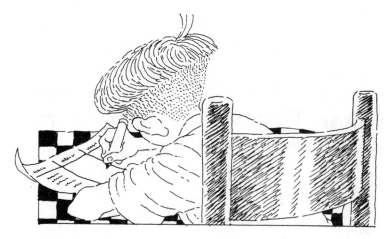

"Hey," shouted Penny. "I'm on your list. What's a suspect?"

"The person who's behind the case of the sinking school spirits."

"I'm sinking, I'm sinking," shrieked Penny, falling to the ground.

Brian looked down at her. "You're too young to know how to make a tape of the Pledge backward," said Brian. He drew a line through her name.

"That's not fair," said Penny. "I should get to be a suspect." She pouted. "I suspect you."

"What does that mean?" asked Brian.

Penny narrowed her eyes. What if he was making charts just to throw her off the scent?

"Don't cross your eyes at me," said Brian. "This is serious. You're too little for charts."

"I bet I could solve it without stupid

charts. Just because I can't write good doesn't mean I wouldn't make an excellent detective."

Brian moved to his next column, "Access." "The person who did it had to have access to Mr. Demert's office."

"What does access mean?" asked Penny. "I bet it's a bad word."

"It is not. It means that the person had the opportunity—you know, like they could get in and out of the principal's office and into your kindergarten class where the cocoons are and they had to know about the cocoons."

"Our kindergarten class is never locked," said Penny. "And everybody knows about our cocoons because we have a chart about them out in the hall. See, kindergartners have charts too."

Brian put his head in his hands. Penny continued to look over his shoulder at the chart. "And Mr. Demert didn't do it," she said.

"How do you know?" asked Brian.

"I just know," said Penny. "He *loves* School Spirit Week!"

Brian sighed. He had to admit Penny was right. Mr. Demert was the biggest booster of School Spirit Week. He would hardly be likely to ruin it at his own school.

"Now your teacher, Mr. Vickers," Penny went on. "He's the type to do it."

Brian stared at her. The truth was Mr. Vickers had been very unenthusiastic about School Spirit Week. "He did call it a tapestry," said Brian, writing "hates School Spirit Week" under "motive" opposite Mr. Vickers's name.

"Mr. Vickers is friends with Ms. Turnaturi," said Penny. "I always see them talking in the hall." Penny put her thumb in the air as if she were counting suspects.

"But then Heather is on your list," continued Penny, sticking up her second finger. "She's our hall monitor. She knows about our butterflies. She said her old school had butterflies and they all hatched."

"Will you stop babbling while I'm working," complained Brian, but he wrote down that Heather had access to the kindergarten classroom.

Penny put her third finger in the air. "Mookie's grandmother collects butterflies. He's always coming in and out checking our cocoons."

"Will you shut up," said Brian.

But he stared at Mookie's name. Mookie had once called School Spirit Week lame. Would that have been reason enough for Mookie to pull off those pranks?

Brian sighed. The more he thought about it, the more Mr. Vickers seemed like the best suspect. A teacher could go in and out of the principal's office whenever he wanted. Mr. Vickers didn't like School Spirit Week, and for all Brian knew he didn't like Mr. Demert.

Brian folded up his chart. He felt bad because he liked Mr. Vickers. Nonetheless, a detective couldn't let his feelings stand in the way of the truth.

Mr. Vickers probably would get fired. He might never get another teaching job again. He might end up homeless, old, and alone.

His mother interrupted Brian's thoughts. "Brian, you're not dressed very nicely. Today is Dress-Up Day. Why don't you wear the tuxedo you wore for Marta's wedding?"

"Why bother?" said Brian. "Why

bother even getting dressed?" The thought of Mr. Vickers homeless really depressed him.

His mother stared at him. "Brian, are you all right?"

"He's just in a bad mood because I'm a better detective than him."

"You haven't detected anything," said Brian.

"I know Mr. Vickers did it," said Penny.

Brian glared at her. That was the exact same conclusion he had come to, but Penny hadn't done any detecting. She was just guessing.

"Come on, Brian," coaxed Mrs. Casanova. "Why don't you change your clothes? I'll go upstairs and help you." Brian did not want his mother helping him get dressed. Maybe he should get dressed up. A real detective might just be wearing a tuxedo when he made his big catch.

When Brian came downstairs, he patted his pocket, where he had put his chart. When they got on the bus, Mookie and Heather were both dressed in tuxedos. "My mom says, 'A woman always looks good in a tuxedo,'" said Heather.

"It's frosty," said Penny.

"Thanks," said Heather.

"Heather, you don't really think the principal would boil the culprit in oil, do you?" asked Penny. "That would be gross."

"No, I'm sure the kid would be kicked out of school," said Heather.

"Would a teacher get kicked out?" asked Penny.

"Mind your own business, Pea Brain," said Brian.

Penny crossed her arms over her chest.

"I hate being called Pea Brain," she said.

"I don't blame you," said Heather. "What's that about a teacher?"

Brian shot Penny a warning look. Penny pretended to seal her mouth and throw away the key.

The bus pulled up to school. Mr. Demert was standing by the buses dressed in a top hat and a blazing white formal suit with tails.

He was singing, "Puttin' on my top hat . . ." As the kids got off the bus, he bowed to each of the boys and kissed each of the girls on the hand.

Penny giggled when he kissed her hand. Mrs. Hamilton had a white carnation for each boy and a red rose for each girl. Even Mr. Vickers had worn a tuxedo. Brian bit his lower lip.

He would watch Mr. Vickers like a hawk. Everywhere that Mr. Vickers went,

Brian would be his shadow.

"This is kind of fun," said Penny, smelling her rose.

"Fun," sniffed Brian. "This isn't a day for fun." He followed Mr. Vickers into class.

And all day everything went smooth as silk. The children all called the teachers "Sir" or "Ma'am" in honor of Dress-Up Day. Every time a teacher came into the class, everyone stood up.

Penny got very tired from jumping up and down all day. Being polite can be exhausting. During recess the boys and girls practiced bowing and curtsying to each other. Penny didn't curtsy very well. She kept falling on her nose.

Meanwhile Brian couldn't believe what a boring day Mr. Vickers was having. He spent his entire free period correcting tests in the front of the classroom.

He never even took a break to go to the bathroom.

"Hey, Brian," said Mookie. "I've got to talk to you about your idea for Animal Hullabaloo."

"Not now, Mook," said Brian. "I'm busy."

Mookie looked a little hurt. Brian stopped. Maybe Mookie was trying to tell him something. When Brian turned back to talk to him, Mookie was gone. Brian tried to find him in the hallway, but so many kids were wearing tuxedos, it was hard to pick him out.

During recess Brian noticed Mr. Vickers talking to Ms. Turnaturi. When it was time for their break, Mr. Vickers walked with Ms. Turnaturi into the teachers' lounge opposite the kindergarten class. Brian tried to follow them. Heather saw Brian lurking in front of the teachers'-lounge door.

"What are you doing here?" she asked.

"Nothing," growled Brian. "Leave me alone."

"You kids in this school are so nasty," muttered Heather as she went back out to the playground.

Brian knew that he couldn't stay in front of the teachers' lounge without an excuse. He sighed and went back out to the playground.

Penny asked him where he had been. "It's none of your business," said Brian.

"Everything is my business," said Penny. "I'm a detective."

Brian shook his head. "Go play your games with someone your own age, Pea Brain. I've got real work to do."

Penny put her hands on her hips. "I'll show you," she said. When the kindergarten class went back in from recess,

Penny and Virginia looked to see how the cocoons were doing.

"This is very weird," said Virginia.

All of the cocoons had little black bow ties made out of black construction paper around their necks.

They looked very dead.

"Ms. Turnaturi," yelled Penny. Ms. Turnaturi came running. She looked down at the cage. She frowned.

"I'm going to have to show this to Mr. Demert," she said. "Class, I want you to sit at your desks and draw pictures for a minute. I'll have the student teacher next door come watch you. I'll be right back."

Penny sat at her desk. She tried to think of something cheerful to draw, but all she could think of was dead butterflies and Brian telling her to mind her own business.

by Tyron

When Ms. Turnaturi came back, she had a scarf draped over the butterfly cage. "We'll keep them under wraps until the celebration tomorrow."

"What did you do with the bow ties?" asked Jenny.

"Mr. Demert and I took them off. He's keeping them."

"Fingerprints," whispered Penny to herself. "What if the culprit left fingerprints?"

"Excuse me, Penny?" asked Ms. Turnaturi.

"Nothing," said Penny quickly.

"Girls and boys, I have something very serious to say to you," said Ms. Turnaturi. "Mr. Demert and I are going to treat you kindergartners as very grown up. We want you to keep what happened a secret. Mr. Demert doesn't want the person who's been fooling with School

Spirit Week to get a chuckle out of this. Can you children keep a secret?"

Penny solemnly crossed her heart.

This was a job for a detective—a detective with a brain, even if it was a pea brain. Ms. Turnaturi had asked them not to say anything about the bow ties. But that didn't mean that she couldn't use her knowledge to do a little detecting on her own.

Meanwhile back in class Brian was getting more and more depressed. The day was almost over and absolutely *nothing* had happened. Brian couldn't believe it. How could he confront Mr. Vickers if nothing happened?

When the bell rang for dismissal, Brian didn't get up from his chair.

"Brian," said Mr. Vickers, "do you want to stay after school and do *more* homework?"

Brian shook his head. "I just can't believe that today was such a calm day," he said.

"Well, that's what happens when people add a little formality to their style," said Mr. Vickers. "I have to admit that today was my favorite day of the week."

Brian wondered if that was an explanation of why nothing had happened. But if Mr. Vickers had liked Dress-Up Day, he would hate Animal Hullabaloo, when everybody in school was invited to dress as their favorite animal. School would be a real zoo. Something really terrible could happen tomorrow.

5

Friday

The Butterflies Flew Free

Mrs. Casanova had bought a face-painting kit for Brian and Penny. Mr. Casanova was a very good artist, so he had the honor of doing the painting. Brian had asked to go as a zebra. Black and white were two of his favorite colors.

"Come on, Penny," said Mr. Casanova. "I'll paint your face too. Maybe you will let me use some colors."

"I like black and white," said Brian. "A

zebra is a very fine animal."

"Black and white aren't real colors," said Penny. "We learned that in kindergarten. I'm very smart for a pea brain."

"Go fly away," said Brian.

"I can't fly."

"I thought you were a butterfly," said Brian. He looked at himself in the mirror. Black and white stripes reminded him of people in jail. Brian didn't have time to fight with Penny. He imagined himself hauling Mr. Vickers into Mr. Demert's office and telling Mr. Demert that he had found the culprit. Mr. Demert would announce over the loudspeaker that Brian was a superior detective. Brian found himself blushing at the thought.

"What's black and white and red all over?" asked Mrs. Casanova.

"A newspaper, Ma," said Brian. "That's the oldest joke in the world."

"I was thinking of a blushing zebra," said Mrs. Casanova. Brian blushed even deeper.

"I want to look like a beautiful butterfly," said Penny.

Mr. Casanova painted the delicate wings of a monarch butterfly on Penny's face.

When they got on the bus, Brian sat next to Mookie. Mookie was dressed like a turtle.

"It's an old Halloween costume," Mookie admitted. "But I like turtles." He was carefully carrying a big trash bag with little holes in it.

Heather was dressed in a feathered mask and a green shirt. "I'm a parrot," she announced.

"Want a cracker?" asked Mookie.

"What do you have in that bag?" Heather asked Mookie. "Let me see."

"It's nothing," said Mookie.

"I bet you have an animal in there that you're going to use to mess up Animal Hullabaloo," said Heather.

Mookie looked at her.

"I'm going to keep my eye on you," said Heather.

They got off the bus. Mr. Demert greeted them dressed as a lion. "I always wanted a mane of hair," he joked. "Good morning, Brian. I like your costume. What's black and white and red all over?"

Brian rolled his eyes. "Maybe I shouldn't have come as a zebra."

Ms. Turnaturi was dressed as a peacock. She smiled at Penny. "You are a very pretty butterfly."

Mr. Vickers was dressed as an American eagle. Mr. Demert sighed when he saw him. "The bald eagle," said Mr. Demert. "Not my favorite bird."

"It's a majestic bird of prey," said Mr. Vickers.

"A bird of prey," repeated Brian to himself.

Mookie looked down at his garbage bag. "I think eagles eat butterflies for snacks," he said.

After lunch all the classes gathered for the "Jungle Walk" in front of the school. The kindergartners were the last ones outside. "Is this where we set the butterflies free?" asked Virginia. Ms. Turnaturi was carrying the cage with a scarf over it.

"Are they really butterflies yet?" asked Penny, not even daring to hope.

"Some of them," said Ms. Turnaturi. She kept the scarf tight over the cage.

Mr. Vickers took Brian's class right next to the kindergartners. "Can I help you with that cage?" Mr. Vickers asked Ms. Turnaturi.

Ms. Turnaturi smiled. "No, I have things firmly in hand," she said.

Brian bit his lip. Was Mr. Vickers trying to get ahold of the cage so he could do something awful to the cocoons?

Penny was glad to be standing near Brian. She saw Mookie carrying his giant garbage bag. It was time to put her pea brain to work being a detective. She even had a plan.

She waited until Ms. Turnaturi was out of earshot. "Hi, guys," she said. "Who do you think put those creepy things around the cocoons?" she said out loud. Ms. Turnaturi had asked them not to mention the bow ties, but if she didn't say the word, she would be keeping the secret.

"What creepy things?" asked Mookie.

Mr. Vickers looked puzzled.

Penny nodded. "The little white

thingamagigs," she said. "You know about them, don't you, Mr. Vickers?"

Brian was ready to kill her. He was planning on catching Mr. Vickers himself, just as soon as he could think of a trap.

"They were black, weren't they?" Heather asked.

Penny stared at her.

"Brian!" she shrieked. Then she stood on her tiptoes so that she could whisper in Brian's ear. Brian couldn't believe it. Pea Brain actually had a brain in her head.

Suddenly Heather ran up to Ms. Turnaturi. She waved her feathers around. "Be careful," Heather warned Ms. Turnaturi. "Brian and Mookie have something up their sleeves."

"What?" asked Ms. Turnaturi. As Ms. Turnaturi's attention was drawn to Brian

and Mookie, Heather took the cocoon cage from her.

"No!" screamed Penny.

Brian flew across the playground and wrapped his arms around Heather. Penny took the cocoon cage and held it gently.

"Get away from me," said Heather.

"You were going to do something to the kindergarten butterflies. You want to sabotage the last day of School Spirit Week," said Brian.

Mr. Demert came running over. "What's going on? Don't tell me it's another school spirit mess-up. Ms. Turnaturi, we're about to begin the ceremony celebrating the end of School Spirit Week."

"We'll be ready in just a minute," said Ms. Turnaturi. "But first I think that Heather had better explain herself."

Heather licked her lips. She swallowed

and looked at the ground. "I hate this school," she blurted out, bursting into tears.

"Heather," said Mr. Demert, not unkindly, "I think you'd better come clean." He put an arm around her shoulder. "Maybe you should tell me exactly what happened."

"You're going to have to kick me out," said Heather. "I knew you'd have to do it. I got the idea when I saw Brian chasing the cat and you got mad. I ruined School Spirit Week. Now you'll have to send me back to my old school."

Mr. Demert and Heather's mother looked at each other. "Young lady, you and I have a lot to talk about," said Mr. Demert.

"You will have to kick me out, won't you?" asked Heather. She sounded as if that's what she hoped would happen.

84

Mr. Demert shook his head. "No, we want you to learn to like Pine Beach. After all, we have the best school spirit. Don't we, Brian and Penny? Heather, I'd like you to go to my office now and wait for me. You and I and your mom will need to have a very long talk. I'm sure that we can find some ways to make you feel more at home at Pine Beach."

Brian took Penny's hand. "Come on," he said quietly. "Let's leave Heather alone with Mr. Demert and her mom. I'll help you find your class."

Penny and Brian wandered among all the kids dressed up as animals.

The kindergarten class was standing near the flagpole. Penny tugged on Ms. Turnaturi's arm. "It's okay," she said. "You can tell me now. The cocoons never hatched—we don't have any butterflies. I know that's true."

"Penny, what are you talking about?" asked Ms. Turnaturi. She picked the scarf off the cage and showed Penny that most of the cocoons had hatched into beautiful monarch butterflies.

Penny grinned. "They look just like me," she said.

Penny went and stood next to Brian. "The butterflies hatched!" she said. "You said they'd never hatch, Brian Brain. And I discovered who did it. You thought it was Mr. Vickers, and you were wrong, wrong, wrong."

"Oh, be quiet, Pea Brain," said Brian. "I was the one who caught Heather."

"Don't call me Pea Brain, not when I just figured out the mystery. And Ms. Turnaturi likes Mr. Vickers. I figured that out. Say, what did you and Mookie have in that bag, anyhow?"

"Nothing," Brian muttered.

"It's something," said Penny.

Mookie slowly opened the garbage bag. It was full of monarch butterflies.

"Where did you get them?" Penny asked.

"I was worried that your butterflies wouldn't hatch," said Brian, "so I asked Mookie to get some extras from his grandmother. Then I got so involved in solving the mystery, I forgot."

"You did that for me?" asked Penny.

Brian sighed. "I did it for the school spirit."

Then Ms. Turnaturi opened the glass cage. Mookie opened his bag. And all of the butterflies flew free.